Brother, Can You Spare a Dime?

Molly Schaar Idle

Abingdon Press

Nashville

Brother, Can You Spare a Dime?

ISBN 13: 978-0-687-49485-9

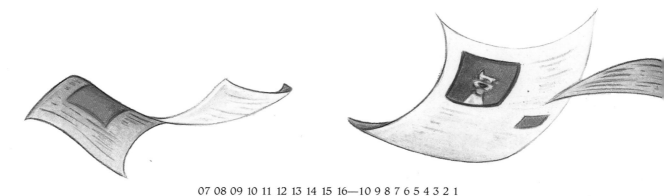

07 08 09 10 11 12 13 14 15 16—10 9 8 7 6 5 4 3 2 1

Printed in China

For Ray
and Judy

FRIDAY

Friday at No. 10 Easy Street dawned brisk, bright, and bustling with activity from top to bottom. And it was just as Sam was untying his stack of newspapers that Mr. Sterling opened the front door.

Everyone who lived on Easy Street tipped their hats and stopped to say hello whenever Mr. Sterling passed by.

He lived on the top floor of No. 10 and could always be found with a twinkle in his eye, an extra chocolate bar in his pocket, and a helping hand for those who needed it.

SATURDAY

On Saturday, Mrs. Churlish's prized begonia made a bid for freedom from the second-floor windowsill and was rescued deftly by Mr. Sterling.

SUNDAY

On Sunday, Mr. Sterling helped
Mr. Fairweather beat a worthy opponent
in a game of chess on the steps of No. 10.

OPPONENT DEMANDS REMATCH

MONDAY

And, on Monday, he gave Sam an extra dime as he paid for his evening newspaper.

No one knew that the next day would be . . .

BLACK TUESDAY

...the day the stock market crashed.

STOCK MARKET
CRASHES!

WEDNESDAY

Overnight, life on Easy Street changed from top to bottom. Mr. Sterling lost everything when the stock market crashed, even his home at No. 10. Without a dime to his name, he was turned out onto the street.

No one stopped to say hello or to tip their hat to him anymore.

Mrs. Churlish bustled past Mr. Sterling on her way home from the florist.

Even Mr. Fairweather put away
his chessboard when he saw
Mr. Sterling coming.

Only Sam remembered the kindness Mr. Sterling had shown him and wanted very much to do something for him in return.

The basement of No. 10 was Sam's home. It was small, and from the outside it looked uninviting. But when Sam opened the door, everything changed; a warm light filled the tiny room. Sharing all that he had, Sam gave Mr. Sterling his last dime, the very dime Mr. Sterling had given to him.

Outside, Mr. Fairweather and Mrs. Churlish could hear the sounds of laughter and see the light from the basement window spilling over onto the sidewalk where they stood.

When Sam opened the door for them, they could feel the light and the warmth.

It was kindness.
It was love.

Love your neighbor as yourself.
Matthew 19:19 (NIV)

The End